This igloo book belongs to:

....

igloobooks

Written by Melanie Joyce
Illustrated by Polona Lovsin

Copyright © 2017 Igloo Books Ltd

Published in 2021
First published in the UK by Igloo Books Ltd
An imprint of Igloo Books Ltd
Cottage Farm, NN6 0BJ, UK
Owned by Bonnier Books
Sveavägen 56, Stockholm, Sweden

Manufactured in China. 1021 001 PK
10 9 8 7 6 5 4

Library of Congress Cataloging-in-Publication
Data is available upon request.

ISBN 978-1-78810-066-3
IglooBooks.com
bonnierbooks.co.uk

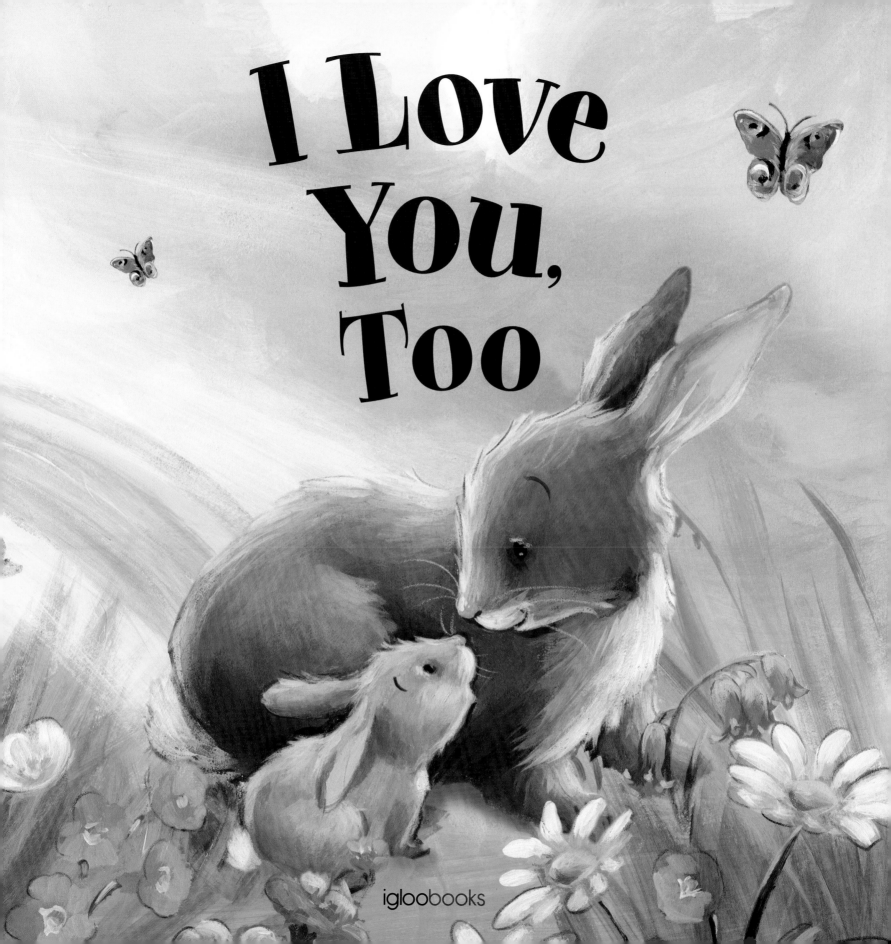

I Love You, Too

igloobooks

You look so cute in the morning all snuggled up in bed,
as sunbeams shine on you, my little sleepyhead.

It makes me feel so happy when you say,
"Mommy, I love you."
Now, I'll tell you all the reasons why
I love you, too.

Sometimes you are
very bouncy and love
to jump around.

"Watch me, Mommy!"
you cry, as you roll
along the ground.

We play hide-and-seek and
splash in puddles, too.

You love to squeal and run away
when I chase after you.

I love you because you want to play, no matter what the weather.

You giggle with your little friends, as you have fun together.

I love you because you say my stories
are the best you've ever heard.

You sit very still, without a sound,
listening to every word.

You give me lovely, squashy hugs, which are as warm as toast.

Your tickly kisses make me giggle and I love them the most.

I love you because you are very brave,
even when you cry.
I dab at your dribbly, trickly tears and
gently wipe them dry.

Sometimes we sit together,
in the evening light.
We watch the pale moon rise,
waiting for the night.

You are the most precious thing to me.
There is no one quite like you.
I know you will always love me and
I will always love you, too.

I love you,

Little Bunny